This fun **Phonics** reader

belongs to

_____

Ladybird Reading

Phonics

BOOK 1

A catalogue record for this book is available from the British Library

Published by Ladybird Books Ltd
80 Strand London WC2R 0RL
A Penguin Company

4 6 8 10 9 7 5 3
© LADYBIRD BOOKS LTD MMVI
LADYBIRD and the device of a Ladybird are trademarks of Ladybird Books Ltd

ISBN-13: 978-1-84646-326-6
ISBN-10: 1-84646-326-2

Printed in Italy

Alphapets

by Mandy Ross
illustrated by Neal Layton

introducing the sounds of the alphabet

Annie has an alligator in her attic.

Aa

Bb

Ben has a buffalo in his bed.

Connie has a camel in her car.

Cc

Dd

Dan has a dinosaur on his desk.

Ellie has an elephant in her engine

Ee

Ff

fish food

fox food

Felix has a fox in his fish tank.

Gita has a gorilla in her garden.

Gg

Hh

Harry has a hamster in his hat.

Izzy has an insect in her ink.

Ii

Jj

Jack has a *jellyfish* in his *jug*.

Katie has a kangaroo in her kitchen

Kk

Ll

Lee has a lion on his lap.

Molly has a monster on her mat.

Mm

Nn

Ned has a newt in his net.

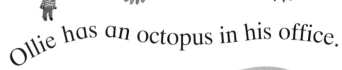

Ollie has an octopus in his office.

Oo

Pp

Penny has a penguin in her pack.

Queenie has a quail on her quilt.

Qq

Rr

Robbie has a rabbit in his rocket.

Sally has a seal on her seesaw.

Ss

Tt

Tom has a tiger in his tent.

Unwin has an umbrella bird in his underwear.

Uu

Vv

Vicky has a vulture in her van.

Wendy has a walrus in her wardrobe

Ww

Xx

Alex has an ox in his box.

Yousef has a yak on his yacht.

Yy

Zz

Zara has a zebra in her zoo.

HOW TO USE
Phonics
BOOK 1

This first book in the **Phonics** series introduces the most common sound made by each letter of the alphabet, and the capital and small letter shapes.

- Have fun reading Alphapets aloud to your child. Familiarity helps children to identify some of the words and phrases.

- Talk about the sounds and pictures together. What sound can your child hear at the beginning of the words?

Phonic puzzles and games are great for learning. See if your child can think of another 'c' pet for Connie, or another 'p' place where Penny could keep her penguin.

Have fun together pairing up each of the children with their alphapet in the scene on pages 30/31.

Phonic fun

Playing 'I spy' games, or tackling tongue twisters together, are fun ways to practise letter sounds.

Help your child put together an alphabet scrapbook of things that begin with the same sound.

Ladybird Reading

Phonics

Phonics is part of the Ladybird Reading range. It can be used alongside any other reading programme, and is an ideal way to practise the reading work that your child is doing, or about to do in school.

Ladybird has been a leading publisher of reading programmes for the last fifty years. **Phonics** combines this experience with the latest research to provide a rapid route to reading success.

The fresh quirky stories in Ladybird's twelve **Phonics** storybooks are designed to help your child have fun learning the relationship between letters, or groups of letters, and the sounds they represent.

This is an important step towards independent reading – it will enable your child to tackle new words by sounding out and blending their separate parts.

How Phonics works

- The stories and rhymes introduce the most common spellings of over 40 key sounds, known as phonemes, in a step-by-step way.

- Rhyme and alliteration (the repetition of an initial sound) help to emphasise new sounds.

- Bright amusing illustrations provide helpful picture clues and extra appeal.